·LIONEL·
IN THE WINTER

·LIONEL· IN THE WINTER

by Stephen Krensky
pictures by Susanna Natti

Dial Books for Young Readers / *New York*

Dial easy-to-read

To Diane and John
S.K.

Remembering
Mary Magna Maletskos
joyfully
S. N.

Published by Dial Books for Young Readers
A Division of Penguin Books USA Inc.
375 Hudson Street
New York, New York 10014

First Edition
1 3 5 7 9 10 8 6 4 2

Library of Congress Cataloging in Publication Data
Krensky, Stephen.
Lionel in the winter / by Stephen Krensky
pictures by Susanna Natti.
p.   cm.
Summary: Lionel's winter adventures include pretending
to be an Arctic explorer, building a snowman, and making
some New Year's resolutions.
ISBN 0-8037-1333-9.   ISBN 0-8037-1334-7 (lib. bdg.)
[1. Winter—Fiction.]   I. Natti, Susanna, ill.
II. Title.
PZ7.K883Lm   1994   [E]—dc20   92–36121   CIP   AC

The full-color artwork was prepared using pencil,
colored pencils, and watercolor washes.
It was then color-separated and reproduced as
red, blue, yellow, and black halftones.

Reading Level 1.9

CONTENTS

A VERY COLD NIGHT

Lionel and his family
were cleaning up after dinner.
"It will be cold tonight,"
said Father.
"I can feel it in my bones."
Lionel frowned.
His bones didn't feel anything.
But he was glad the weather
was changing.
He always liked winter.

Mother looked out the window.

Clouds were passing over the moon.

"The snow is coming," she said.

"Hooray!" said Lionel.

He was excited.

Lionel's sister Louise buttoned

her sweater.

"How much snow will we get?"

she asked.

"So much," said Lionel,

"that the whole house will be covered."

Father made sure the window

was shut tight.

"At least the days will start
getting longer soon," he said.
"And the sun will shine brighter."
"Maybe," said Lionel.
"But on some days the temperature
will drop so low, even the sun
will turn blue from the cold."

Mother rubbed her hands together.

"Still," she said,

"spring will be here before we know it."

"Not so fast," said Lionel.

"The storms in March are the worst.

They freeze our words into icicles

as soon as we say them."

Louise shivered.

"I need another sweater," she said.

She ran upstairs.

"And don't forget the snowball fights,"
said Lionel. "When the snow gets up
your sleeves and down your back."

Father stood up.

"I'd better make sure

we have enough blankets," he said.

He left the kitchen.

"And what about the freezing winds?"
asked Lionel.
"The ones that turn puddles
into sheets of ice."
"I think I'll go check the gloves
and mittens," said Mother.
She went out too.

Lionel looked around the empty room
and sighed.
There was only one bad thing
about winter, he thought.
Sometimes it got a little lonely.

THE EXPLORER

Lord Lionel Showshoe,

the Arctic explorer,

was crossing the frozen snow.

Nine strong huskies were pulling

his dogsled.

A storm had been raging for days.

Most explorers would have gotten

hopelessly lost.

But not Lord Lionel.

He kept his bearings.

"There's the North Pole," he said.

"I'd know it anywhere."

Suddenly he heard the sound

of rushing snow.

"Avalanche!" he cried.
Lord Lionel ducked down
and covered his head.
He hoped the avalanche
wouldn't bury him too deeply.

Luckily he always carried a shovel
in his pack.
It was important to be prepared
for the unexpected.
The Arctic was filled with dangers.
Lord Lionel stood up.

The avalanche had been a small one.

He brushed the snow off his shoulders
and looked around.

"Uh-oh," he said. "Grizzly bears!"

If they saw him, he was doomed.

Lord Lionel backed away slowly.

Suddenly he stopped.

A great crack had opened in the snow.

"From a recent earthquake," he said.

He could not go around it.

Lord Lionel looked down.

He could not see the bottom.

"I'll have to jump across," he said.

There was no time to waste.

The crack could widen at any moment.

Lord Lionel released his huskies

so that they could jump across

by themselves.

Then he backed up

and took a great leap.

He landed safely on the other side.

"Lionel, time to eat,"
said the quartermaster
from his base camp.
The explorer sighed.
It was good to hear a friendly voice
after weeks of traveling in the wilderness.
"Coming," he said,
and went inside for lunch.

THE NEW YEAR

It was the last night of the year.

Father and Mother were out

with some friends.

Louise and the babysitter

were watching a New Year's Eve

party on television.

TOOOT! TOOOOT!

The babysitter jumped up.

"What was that?" she asked.

Louise covered her ears.

"That's Lionel," she sighed.

TOOOOT! TOOOOT!

Lionel came around the corner.

He was blowing a giant horn.

He had made it himself.

"What do you think?" Lionel asked.

"I'm welcoming the new year."

Louise groaned.

The babysitter smiled weakly.

"I'm sure the new year

feels very welcome," she said.

Lionel started to blow again.

"Wait, Lionel," Louise said quickly.

"Maybe you should work
on your resolutions next."

Lionel lowered his horn.

"What are resolutions?" he asked.

Louise sighed. "They're promises
you make to yourself.
It's how everyone starts the new year."

"Promises about what?" asked Lionel.

"Different things," said Louise.

"Like doing your homework

or being nice to people."

She smiled extra sweetly.

"Should I suggest some for you?"

"Okay," said Lionel.

Louise thought for a moment.

"Always do what I tell you," she said.

"And stay in your room

when my friends come over."

"Hmmm," said Lionel.

"I can think of some for you too.

Share your toys with me.

The good ones, I mean.

Don't hog the phone so much.

Eat my vegetables

when nobody's looking.

Help me with the tricky zipper

on my jacket.

Don't pretend your back is hurt

when it's time to shovel the snow.

Stop picking the pepperoni

off our pizzas.

Try to—"

"LIONEL!" Louise shouted.

The babysitter was laughing.

"What?" asked Lionel.

"I think you should blow your horn

some more," she said.

"I think the new year would like that."

Lionel looked pleased.

"Really?" he said.

Louise nodded.

"Okay," said Lionel.

"But remember what I said."

TOOOT! TOOOOT!

Lionel blew his horn

all over the house.

He was glad Louise had taught him

about resolutions.

And if she took his advice,

this would be the best new year yet.

THE SNOWMAN

Lionel was building a snowman
with his friend Jeffrey.
The snowman was made of
three balls of snow.
There was a big ball at the bottom,
a medium ball in the middle,
and a small ball on top.

Lionel pulled a potato

out of his pocket.

"I'll use this for a nose," he said.

"A potato?" said Jeffrey.

"Don't most people use carrots?"

"Yes," said Lionel,

"but I think more people have noses

like potatoes."

Lionel picked up two branches.

"These will be the arms," he said.

"They even have fingers at the end."

"What about the eyes?"

Jeffrey asked.

"I brought these two marbles,"

said Lionel.

He put them in carefully.

Then he added a hat and a scarf.

"Aren't those yours?"

asked Jeffrey.

Lionel nodded. "Only the best

for my snowman," he said.

Then he stepped back.

"You know, he looks kind of familiar."

Louise opened the window.

"Lionel!" she yelled out,

"you're pointing the snowman

the wrong way. He's supposed to

face the street."

"That's silly," Lionel yelled back.

"There's nothing for him
to look at in the street.
There's a lot more for him
to see in our house."
Louise shook her head
and shut the window.
"Besides," Lionel said to Jeffrey,
"if he's facing the house,
he can help guard it."

"Guard it?" said Jeffrey.

"From what?"

Lionel pointed to the fence.

"Maybe tigers," he said.

Jeffrey nodded. "But fighting tigers could be dangerous," he said.

"You're right," said Lionel.

He ran inside and came out again.

"That's better," he said.

Jeffrey shivered.

"Can we go inside soon?" he asked.

"Sure," said Lionel.

He looked at the snowman.

"Do you think he'll be lonely

out here by himself?"

"I don't know," said Jeffrey.

"But there's nothing

we can do about that.

We can't bring him inside with us."

"That's true," said Lionel.

"But we can still help."

A short time later

Lionel and Jeffrey

went inside for cocoa.

The snowman stayed outside,

but he wasn't lonely at all.

ML